FOUR DAYS AND THREE NIGHTS

by

L. WILLIAMS

Forward by Tricia Hayles

It's been my pleasure to know Lydell Williams over the past five years. We have gone from being mere acquaintances to having a great friendship. When he initially approached me with his first draft, I was thoroughly surprised that he had taken on this endeavor. Upon reading I was instantly taken in by the storyline and characters. I encouraged him to continue because I really wanted to see where it would go and I knew that many others would feel the same way.

Lydell reluctantly agreed. What I like about Lydell is his ability to step out of his comfort zone and allow himself to be honestly critiqued. I hope you enjoy his debut novel as much as I did.

Great day to you my dear readers. I hope this book finds you well. My name is Ethan Troutland and this is my story about some of my friends and I. Each of us are in love with someone outside of what society considers a "normal" relationship.

Here's a little about myself. I am 39, married with no kids and I have my master's in aerospace engineering. I work for NASA as an engineer. I live in Houston. The story I am sharing with you is about a lady I met, and ...this is the story of us.

We first crossed paths at a networking event in Houston about 5 years ago. A typical yearly aerospace conference with monotone speakers, cheesy give-a-ways and terrible food. It happened during afternoon intermission. This time the conference hotel had a few bars. I saw a bar off in the distance with one lady sitting there and decided to get my drink from that bar.

I walked up to the bar and she had her glass of white wine in hand. I really didn't have a taste for anything, so I just asked the bartender to give me what she was having. (Pointing to the woman in front of me sheepishly.)

She looked at me and then down at my shoes and said, "good choice". I smiled at her and asked, "Were my shoes a good choice or the wine?" She grinned and said, "All three". "Three?" I repeated with surprise. She said, "You chose to come over here and most men wouldn't". I asked her name. She said, "Elise Kennedy". I introduced myself as Ethan. Her name sounded familiar, but I couldn't quite put my finger on it. She asked me to sit with her over in the corner and to skip the rest of the afternoon sessions.

I laughed and sat down. I did not want to go back in there anyway and for some reason I felt like I would learn more out here. Elise was about five foot nine, with brown skin, shoulder length hair and had the shape of someone who plays tennis. Not bad on the eyes. What seemed like 15 minutes turned out to be 2 hours. The lobby had long since emptied out, and we were on our 3rd glass of wine. We were not really flirting with each other, just enjoying each other's company. We mostly talked about the aerospace industry and where we thought it was headed. I noticed her wedding ring and asked her how long she had been married.

Elise responded with a long sigh and said, "Too long." and we both chuckled. I responded that I had just celebrated my 8th year of marriage last month. Elise told me she had been married 14 years but then immediately asked me "How do you make it work?" I responded, "I don't". We both belted out a laugh. Elise asked me where my wife and I met and then asked to see a picture of her. I showed her one of our anniversary pictures. I told her we met during my sophomore year at NC A&T. She looked up at the pic and said, "Oh, she's pretty. Where is she from?" I told her my father in-law is black and originally from Alabama and my mother in-law is from Thailand. Elise looked at her watch and suggested that we go our separate ways before the crowd let out and handed me her card.

I knew her name rang a bell. I applied at her company in Atlanta about 10 years ago. She was one of the top executives. I did not have a card on me, so Elise put my number in her cell and texted me. She said to stay in touch and pulled a handful of other business cards out of her purse and dropped them in the trash. She told me she was glad she met me and walked away.

Fast forward four years, several conferences together, at least a dozen weekend getaways in each other's city, and one failed weeklong vacation together. We fell in love with each other. We are both still married and have successfully managed to keep our secret to ourselves all this time. It has not been as hard as we thought it would be. With us both being in the same industry, the conferences are easy to set up. We even made up a conference a few times. The calls and texts don't sound an alarm because we both talk a lot between those cities for our work anyway. She has a small team out in Houston so that works for her as well.

I am originally from Atlanta, so going home for the weekend doesn't ring a bell for my wife and her flying out to Houston seems normal to her husband. My wife is from Thailand. She comes from a family of ten, so she loves being at home and enjoying silence while I am away. She helped raise four younger siblings. We have no kids and I got a vasectomy shortly after we married. She says that she was a parent at an early age and is done with that. I come from a family of six and I am the oldest. I have seven nieces and five nephews. I love being the "cool uncle". Us deciding not to have kids was not a deal breaker when we talked about getting married.

Elise has one daughter from a previous marriage, who is about to graduate from high school and go off to Spelman. Her first husband was killed in a car crash by a drunk driver when her daughter was around three years old. Her current husband is about seven years older than her and owns the second largest garbage and recycling company in Atlanta. They are considered a power couple in Atlanta. The networking and charity events that they put on are amazing. Elise is a very well-connected woman, but very humble at the same time. I absolutely love how she is always giving back to the community.

Other than Elise and I being lovers and friends, she has also been a great mentor to me. She convinced me to stay on my job when things got a bit hairy and I wanted to leave. She told me to stay and have them pay for my doctorate degree and pushed me to finish it asap so I could leave them in a much better position and not have any debt.

Here we are now. I have my doctorate degree in hand, and everything is well. I was promoted a few times while at NASA and it's time to celebrate with a much-needed vacation. I want to take a vacation with Elise. I know some of you are asking yourself how the hell are you going to pull off a vacation with her?

Well, I tell you when the universe hears your prayer it

answers. Maybe not how you want the Universe to answer, but it does. The week after I got my Doctorate, my wife surprised me with a trip to see her parents in Thailand to show off her new Ph.D. husband. It was a great trip. We saw a lot of the country and her family was very proud of me.

On the other side of the world. Elise's husband was so busy with running the company that he had not been paying her much attention. He was very "hands on" with his company, but "hands off" where Elise was concerned. Elise was at her wits end and needed to get away. Elise asked him to be home more, but it fell on deaf ears. In public they were envied by most, but in private they hardly spoke. He was very hands on at work, but when it came time to do stuff around the house, he would always tell her to find a handyman or a contractor. Elise's first husband did a lot of the chores and loved fixing stuff around the house and Elise missed that.

Elise loves the fact that I would tell her I just fixed the sink, put up a fan or cut the grass. Working with my hands is like meditation to me. Elise loves putting her fingers between mine and rubbing my hands. We enjoy the passion and chemistry that our relationship has when we get together.

A week after I got back from Korea I received a call from a corporate recruiter. He asked me if I would be interested in being the Director of Operations at a new Aerospace company in Atlanta. I was intrigued to say the least. We had been in Houston for a while. A change of scenery plus being closer to Elise wouldn't hurt.

The recruiter and his team decided to have my interview at TopGolf in Atlanta. Long story short, they offered me a lucrative contract. I would have flight benefits on the private jet they flew me out on. They would also pay the balance of what I owed to NASA for my doctorate program. "How could I turn this down?" I asked myself on the flight back home. I talked it over with my wife and we agreed it was a great opportunity. I also talked to Elise about it and she said that company is likely to be her direct competitor in a few years. She also said that it's a huge industry and we could both eat.

After a few more zoom calls and back and forth on the particulars, I accepted the position in Atlanta. I told them I needed about a month to find a place in Atlanta. A few days later Elise called me and said, "Tell your wife you are doing a guy's trip to Casablanca." Another voice on the phone said "I need some information

Ethan". I raised my voice a little and asked "Who is on the line with us?" Elise said, "Kiesha, my travel agent is sending us to Casablanca." Kiesha had been her friend since high school, and she knew about our situation. Kiesha would make sure everything looked legit on the itinerary so no one would get suspicious.

One of Elise's closest friends ,Kellita , and her boyfriend joined us on vacation. Kiesha assured me that everything on this trip would be taken care of. All I had to do was get to the plane on time. She had been to Casablanca last year and spoke highly of it. Elise could not wait to go.

This was our window to be with each other in public and enjoy ourselves at a location where none of our other friends had been before. I doubt we will see anyone we both know there. I cannot wait.

I flew into Atlanta two days earlier to meet with my cousin who is a real estate agent and look at some homes. We went to see a few but none got my attention. I rented a Slingshot for us and we rode all around town, saw some family and went to a few cigar bars.

It was departure day and cloudy out. I was standing outside Hartsfield International Terminal and thought to myself how this vacation together was long overdue. I saw an Uber XL had just dropped Elise off. Elise and I decided to wait till we got to the gate to really get close to each other. Atlanta is a big little town and we both knew a lot of people here. We didn't want to risk getting caught. We loved the discretion and secrecy of our relationship.

I decided to let a few people get between us going through security. Elise had her hair in a ponytail that I loved, dark slacks, a tan thin sweater and a necklace I got her from my last trip to Jamaica. I tried not to stare at her, but I couldn't help it. We got on the tram and I sat across from her. Elise crossed her legs and looked up at me and grinned. We got off the tram together and headed to our gate. Our flight was on time and we grabbed a seat in the corner. As Elise sat down, I bent down and softy kissed her cheek. She smelled like fresh mangos.

About 10 minutes later we saw her friend Kellita and her boyfriend. Kellita and Elise hugged, then she grabbed me in for a hug. Kellita and I met a few years ago when I came home during the summer. She's trustworthy and liked me more than

Elise's husband. I think that's why she keeps our relationship secret.

Kellita introduced me to her boyfriend Mack. Elise and Kellita started talking about some reality show they had been watching and Mack motioned for me to walk with him. He said he needed to get a drink before the flight because it calmed him down. Mack was about 6 foot 2, muscular, bald headed with a huge ass beard. After a few minutes, I got a good vibe from Mack. He seemed like a cool dude. We ended up just watching a baseball game that was on at the bar. After a few beers we heard our flight being called. We are all in first-class and Mack and Kellita were behind us across the aisle. We pushed out from the gate, Elise grabbed my hand, took off her shoes and rested her head on my shoulder. I put my arm around her and rubbed her back. Elise kissed me on my cheek then leaned back and put on her headphones. I pulled out my tablet and looked for a movie to watch.

One layover in Paris and three hours later we were in Casablanca. We got through security and I saw our driver holding a sign with my last name. She led us to the limo van, offered us hot towels and bottled water. We stretched out in it the back of the limo. Elise laid between my legs and put my arms around her chest. It was a long flight and we both couldn't wait to take a shower, change clothes, grab a drink and relax on the beach.

We pulled up to the resort and the concierge offered us champagne, took our bags and escorted us to our rooms. Elise's travel agent Kiesha had impressed me so far. Everything was smooth and five star all the way. Our rooms were next to each other and we had great views of the beach and sunset. I got some ice to keep my beers cold and headed out to the balcony. Elise headed to the shower.

A few minutes later Elise came out onto the balcony in a robe. She smelled like mangos. She came behind me and rubbed my shoulders. I felt her breasts press into my back. She kissed my back and ran her hand down my chest into my pants. She turned me around and kissed me and put her hands down my pants. I walked her backwards to a lounge chair and laid her down. Her robe opened to reveal an ebony goddess.

I put my beer down, grabbed the back of her knees and spread her legs wide. I kissed, sucked and licked all of her. She moaned when I pulled on her clit with my lips. I grabbed her waist and pulled her closer to me. I cupped her breasts and pulled on her clit with my lips as I looked up at her. Elise bit her lip and ran her fingers thru my hair. I put my hand on the small of her back so she wouldn't squirm so much. She grinded her pussy into my chin. Up, down, and in circles. It would be just a few more moments before she climaxed. Elise started to moan. I could hear her muscles contract. Her back cracked as she had her first orgasm.

I know her very well so I covered her mouth with one hand and twisted her nipples softly with the other so no one would hear moaning. I grabbed some ice and put it on her throbbing clit. She almost knocked me off the lounge chair. I moved the ice from her clit up to her breasts while I kept licking her pussy. She grabbed my hand and started sucking on my fingers. That made me suck and lick her even harder. I grabbed her waist with both my hands and when she came this time I couldn't cover her mouth in time. She let out a seductive yet loud moan. If anyone was within shouting distance, I know they had to have heard it.

Just then there was a knock at the door. "WTF??!!" I said to myself. Another three knocks. I didn't think it would stop so I went to the door and asked, "Who is it?" It was Mack telling me that we had dinner reservations in 20 minutes and to make sure my lady was ready. I yelled back, "OK!"

I walked back out to the balcony with my dick harder than freezer meat. Elise was already turned over with her ass in the air, so I thrust myself in. Elise gripped the lounge chair tight and told me to go harder. I went as deep as I could. I started hearing that macaroni sound. I could feel myself touch the deepest part of her. Elise could tell I was about to cum and jumped off me and grabbed me. I came on her chest and she licked the cum dripping from me.

We met Kellita and Mack downstairs for a burlesque dinner show. The performers were very entertaining. I had never been to a burlesque show. The drinks and food were amazing as well. We all had a great time. I may have to find one in Atlanta when I get back.

The next morning, I thought about our first day there and how outstanding it was. We had a VIP reception, some great sex, a nice dinner and show. After dinner we all walked down to the beach and watched the stars.

I left the balcony door open last night and the sound of the ocean woke me up. I looked over at Elise's tanned shoulders. I tried not to wake her, but she rubbed her feet against my leg. She grabbed my hand to let me know she was awake.

A lazy day was on the schedule for day two. No spa treatments or excursions planned on purpose. I put the "DO NOT DISTURB" sign on the door last night when we came in just in case housekeeping decided to get an early start. The sun was shining through the curtains over her head. I moved to get up, but She grabbed my hand and moved it over her chest to pull me closer. I kissed her brown shoulders and she pushed her ass to me. Her hair still smelled good, like a mix between mangos and the ocean. I ran my hand down her side and we interlocked fingers. This non-verbal way of communicating suited us best because we both talk to people all day long at work. I grabbed her ass with both hands as she rubbed my back.

The sun reflected off the marble floor and into my eyes and she told me she loved my brown eyes. Her nipples rubbed against my chest and stomach as she kissed me. I grabbed her hips and she forced my hands to my side. She put one hand on my chest and grabbed my throbbing dick with the other and slowly slid me into her. Up a little, down a little, then all the way down. She went slowly at first, taking me all the way in with every stroke. Her breasts came together between her arms with every stroke. I dared not to move as she went faster and faster. Elise put my hand on her clit to rub it as she grinded on top of me. Elise fell on top of me as she dug into the bed. A few moments later she came. Her head fell forward onto my shoulder and her hair went over my face. I rolled over and put her on her back. I pushed back her legs and ate her out till she came again. I thrusted into her while she was having her second orgasm and it took her breath away. She took a deep breath and put her hand on my stomach so I wouldn't go deeper. I moved her hand and she reached around for a pillow to scream in. I continued to go deep with every stroke a she moaned into the pillow. I grabbed her shoulders and came inside of her and she moved her hips back and forth on me.

I laid next to her. The sun was shining on her sweaty body. We both didn't move for a few minutes. Her sweaty body shined in the sunlight.

Both of us tried to catch our breath, then Elise wiped sweat from my forehead and said, "Good Morning".

She got out of bed and saw Kellita had texted her a few times. They wanted us to go to breakfast with them. "Well, we obviously missed those messages" Elise said. We showered together and got dressed. Moments later, Kellita knocked on the door. I let her in. Kellita looked me up and down and grinned then sat in the desk chair and talked to Elise. Mack stuck his head in then held up two cigars and motioned for me to come out.

Mack was really laid back and cool. We went downstairs to one of the bars. There was some eye candy walking around that gave us a little something to chat about. We ordered a few beers and headed outside to look for a spot to enjoy the cigars and for people to watch. We both knew these women would not come soon.

Mack passed me a cigar and a lighter then held up his beer to me. He asked me where I met Elise. I told him how we met at a conference and hit it off. I told him about how we met again in the airport after that conference was over.

I was scheduled to go to Philadelphia after the conference where I first met Elise. I ended up sleeping late and missed my flight. I was at the gate taking a nap and Elise nudged my shoulder. She was on my next flight available which had a layover in Atlanta. We sat there in the terminal and talked for about an hour. I had the bright idea to ask her where she was sitting, and did she mind if I joined her. She perked up and went to the gate attendant. They talked and laughed like they had known each other for years and then she came back with my new boarding pass. It was first class. I asked her how much I owed her, and she said I already paid for it with the conversation. She told me that the gate attendant was a sorority sister and she hooked her up since the flight wasn't fully booked. It was at that moment that I knew I had to get to know her better.

Elise sat by the window, took off her shoes and asked for a blanket. She grabbed my hand and asked if she could put her head on my shoulder during the flight. Mack stopped me and said, "I think she had a plan buddy" and we both laughed.

Mack started talking about how he met Kellita. Mack said they first met at her family reunion. Mack owns a catering business in Atlanta and Kellita's aunt contracted him to be the caterer for their family reunion. Mack said it wasn't his first family reunion, but it was his largest yet. He was supervising the breakfast and overheard Kellita say that she wished they had more crispy bacon. He wanted to be the best caterer possible, so he went back to the kitchen and made more bacon.

Mack said Kellita looked surprised and happy when he took her the bacon. Mack said he told her he overheard her talk about the bacon. "The cousins and aunts that were at the table started eyeing me bro!" Mack said. Mack said he may have saw her one other time that day but didn't think of it as a big deal. He had to get back to make sure everything was going okay and then get ready for the lunch service.

The next day at breakfast Kellita stopped Mack and asked for another plate of bacon. Mack took that as a flirt and started to head back to the kitchen. Kellita's aunt walked up, grabbed him by the arm and introduced him to Kellita as the caterer. Mack said Kellita perked up.

Mack said a few weeks after the reunion he got an email from Kellita. She wanted to come by his office and talk about getting a quote. This was something Mack could have done over the phone or via his website. He said he agreed to and he would be available that Friday after 5pm. Mack took a big gulp of his beer and said "Bruh, Kellita had a plan. I didn't see it at the time, but she had a plan for me."

The Kellita I knew was very blunt and talked to everyone like she has known them for years. She told Mack that she needed him to prepare a three-course meal for an awards ceremony. She wanted to come in for a tasting.

That Friday she came to Mack's office a little late. Mack saw her pull in and checked her out from the window. Mack said he liked what he saw. She had on a dark knee-length skirt, blouse, and jacket. Mack walked her around his facility. She seemed genuinely interested and asked some questions. He took her back to his conference room for the tasting and asked her if she wanted a glass of wine to go with the meal. She declined so Mack brought her some water. She asked if he was going to join her and he told her he had to finish up some stuff in the back and would be back soon. Mack still had a few employees getting things ready for an event the next day.

Mack came back and she said, "I enjoyed it and I'm looking forward to the next course." Mack said he tried not to stare at her, but he couldn't help himself. Mack said Kellita was his type of woman. Mack reached for her plate and noticed her cleavage. He told her he would join her for the rest of the meal once everyone was gone.

When Mack came back to the conference room, he saw that her jacket was off. Her blouse was a little more open. "She didn't have a bra on. Her nipples were poking thru her shirt and her legs were uncrossed towards me." Mack said. She smiled at him and stroked his arm as he put her plate down. "She had a plan!" Mack exclaimed.

Mack said she leaned in with every bite to make sure Mack could see down her blouse. She leaned back so he could see her nipples press against her shirt. Kellita asked Mack if his crew was still in the building. "Man, I got my ass up and checked every room to make sure we were alone." Mack blurted. Mack came back to the room and she had already closed the blinds and asked again if everyone was gone. Mack said "Yes" and closed the door behind him. She grabbed his hand and pulled Mack into her.

She took off her blouse, lifted up her skirt and laid on the table. She told me that my dick better be worth every bit of the $10,000 she was about to spend. I tried to suck out of her soul. When she stopped shaking, I flipped her over and gave her $10,010 worth of dick. I didn't last long but it was enough for her. She laid there like she was just pinned by Ric Flair. She stumbled to the restroom to straighten up and when she came back, she asked me, "Why you?" I told her, "I ask no questions, I get told no lies."

Kellita said she wanted to fuck me ever since the reunion. She liked the way I handled myself around her horny aunts and cousins who were basically throwing the pussy at me during the reunion. She had to play it cool at the reunion because her husband was there. He was the real jealous type and she knew if she looked at me too hard then he would cause a scene. For the last two years I have been serving up Kellita almost weekly at my office.

We heard giggling from the bar area and looked up and saw our lovely ladies with huge drinks in hand. Mack and I were already buzzed from the cigars and beers. We walked to where we were having a private lunch. A staff member greeted us at the beach and showed us to our private area. Elise's travel agent Kiesha was the best. I would have never thought of this stuff if it were up to me.

We walked down the beach. The water was calm and clear. We could see the ocean floor at least forty yards away. There were two cabanas with queen sized mattresses in them and two lounge chairs in front of each of them. In the middle of the cabanas was a table already set up with water, juices and fruit slices.

The waiter took our drink orders and handed us all beach towels. Mack and Kellita strolled out into the water. Elise and I sat down at the table. I pulled out Elise's chair and kissed her lips. She took my legs and rubbed them.

Mack and Kellita came out of the water about 20 minutes later and sat at the table with us just in time for the food and drinks to arrive. There were three waiters in front of us. One with our drinks, and the other two with two huge platters. They put the platters down and removed the lids. One was full of shrimp, lobster tails, oysters and king crab legs. The other platter had fresh local fish, ribeye steaks and chicken.

After we ate, Mack and Kellita headed back into the water. Elise and I got our lounge chairs and pulled them to the edge of the water. The waves hitting or legs made both of us doze off.

I woke up to the sounds of a bed rocking. Our friends were getting it in behind us. Elise grabbed my chin, kissed my lips then looked back at them. She smiled at me and grabbed my hand. She led me further out into the water. We waded out about waist deep. A turtle swam and colorful fish swam past us. We walked a little bit further till the water was chest high. Elise stopped and faced me. If the world ended, I would have been just fine dying in her arms.

Elise pushed her hair back and wrapped her arms around me. I grabbed her hips and kissed her neck. Elise moved her hands down my back and up my chest. She then untied my swim trunks. She rubbed me with one hand and untied her bikini bottom with the other. Elise put her bikini bottom around my neck and told me to pick her up. Elise had one hand on my shoulder and then she put me inside of her. Even in this warm water I could tell the difference between her warmth and the water. Elise's forehead was against mine as she looked me in the eye and told me to just hold her steady. The sun was setting over Elise's shoulders as she rode me in rhythm with the waves.

Elise was going up and down on me in perfect rhythm with the ocean. Her hands gripped my back tight as she pressed her head into my shoulder. I kept my balance. We came together before the sun set. Wherever and whenever Elise wanted me, I was willing to give myself to her without question.

We walked back to the cabana and watched the moon as we sipped our drinks. Mack and Kellita motioned us to go back to our rooms and get changed so we could see what the local nightlife looked like.

We all met again downstairs. Elise talked to the concierge about the local nightlife. He called us a van to take us around for the night. We all looked great. Elise had on some shorts and a crop top, no bra, and a necklace I gave her from a business trip I took in Brazil. Kellita was wearing shorts as well with a thin t-shirt. Mack had on linen pants and a matching button down. I had on a polo shirt and linen shorts. We had the concierge to take pictures of just Mack and I.

The van pulled up to a club and we heard the music before we got out of the van. It was an open-air club right on the beach. We walked in the club and were immediately hit by lots of smoke and a weird smell. Elise was not having it and pointed us all back to the van. Elise pulled the driver to the side as we got back in. He drove about 10 minutes up the road to another club. It was also right on the beach and had a large patio. We walked into a better atmosphere with no smoke and no weird smells. A waitress led us to a table right by the patio. We ordered some drinks and the ladies got up and headed to the dance floor. Mack and I hung out just watching people. There was a nice breeze coming off the beach. The music was nice.

    Mack tapped me on the leg and pointed out some lady looking our way. She was cute as hell I thought to myself. Mack motioned for her to come over to us. I told Mack that I did not want to be on an episode of "Locked up Abroad" and then looked around to see where our ladies were. Mack laughed and said, "It's cool". The lady came over and started speaking Spanish to Mack. To my surprise Mack was fluent in Spanish. Mack and the lady were laughing and I happened to look up to see Elise and Kellita looking at us. I looked over to Mack. He was unaware of what I think was a dangerous situation. I looked up again and Kellita and Elise are on the way over to us.

Elise sat next to me and sipped her drink while Kellita sat on Mack's lap as he and the lady chatted. Elise giggled then leaned back on me. I asked Elise, "What's funny?" She told me I needed to learn Spanish. Kellita then started to lap dance on Mack. I said to Mack, "Well what's up?" Mack laughed and said, "That lady is one of my former clients Alba".

Juvenile's 'Back That Ass Up' came on and Elise dragged me to the dance floor. She found a spot, turned around and started grinding on me. I'm looking down at her shirt while she had one hand on my shoulder and one hand in my shorts. That song does something to her whenever it plays. We danced to a few more songs and went to the bar to get some more drinks.

I turned around and saw Alba sitting on Kellita's lap this time. She had her hand on her thigh and Mack was laughing at Alba a little too hard in my opinion. I thought to myself that

Mack just talked himself into a threesome.

A few more drinks and dances and we were nice and lit. It was around 1 am and Mack suggested that we head back to the hotel. We all went out to the patio to enjoy the breeze. We were all sweaty from dancing so the breeze felt nice. We stumbled back to the van then back to the hotel.

When we got up to our room, Elise told me to get in the shower with her. I tried to have sex with her in the shower, but she didn't want to. She told me to follow her out to the deck and get in the plunge pool with her. We both walk out naked, still dripping wet. To my surprise, Alba from the club was already in the pool, naked. Elise went in first and waded over to our guest. Alba smiled at me and motioned for me to come over to them. Alba's body was amazing, she had tan lines that led around her large brown nipples and down to her waist. Elise rubbed my shoulders and they both kissed me. Elise jumped out the pool and sat in a lounge chair. She motioned me to sit on the edge of the pool between her legs. Alba rubbed Elise's legs while kissing my chest. Her breasts rubbed against my dick and she went up and down my chest. Alba put her hair back in a pony tail and started giving me head. Elise ran her fingers thru my hair and leaned over my shoulder to watch. Elise's soft breasts pressed on my back as Alba ran her tongue up and down my dick. Elise scooted back a little and started to pleasure herself. I would look over my shoulder at Elise, and then look down at Alba's breasts going in and out the water almost drowning out the slurping sound she's making on me. I reached down and grabbed Alba's long nipples as I came. Alba didn't back up, she took all of me in her mouth and swallowed. Elise had moved the chair so she could see better and came right after I did.

I got in the pool and pulled Elise closer to the pool's edge and started to eat her out. It didn't take long for her to have a second orgasm. Alba handed both of us a bottle of water and walked back into the room. Elise said she remembered us talking about our fantasies. She said she couldn't bring herself to having a full threesome with me but she didn't mind watching. We got out of the pool and sat in our lounge chairs naked and watched the stars.

"How lucky am I?" I thought to myself.

We woke up the next morning to the noise of the maid coming in. I asked her to just clean the shower and give us fresh towels. Elise rolled over and faced me, wrapped one arm and a leg around me, and dug her head into my chest. I rubbed her back in circles making sure I rubbed her butt like she liked. The maid gasped. Maybe she thought we were about to have sex in front of her, but we weren't. Just two people so into each other that nothing else mattered around us. The maid cleaned the bathroom in a hurry and left the towels. We laid on each other for a few more minutes then I put on a robe and went on the balcony.

I saw a yoga class going on at one of the pool areas. On the other side of the balcony I saw a family with small kids setting up on the beach. The dad chased his toddler towards the ocean, scooped him up, and dipped his feet in the water. The temperature was around 90 degrees with no clouds. I went back in and grabbed my phone and saw I had a text from my wife. She asked for pictures of the resort. I sent a picture of myself on the balcony. I told her that Mack and I went out to a few clubs and got drunk. She asked for more pictures. I scrolled through my phone. I checked and rechecked my pictures to make sure there was nothing in the background that would give me away. Everything looked good so I sent her a few more.

Elise came out to the balcony wearing her cover-up and told me that Kiesha planned horseback riding and a sunset dinner cruise for our last day.

We met Mack and Kellita downstairs at the van that would take us horseback riding. Elise looked over at Kellita and asked did she have a cover up or another shirt she could put on. Her outfit wasn't exactly horseback riding friendly. Mack laughed. Kellita responded with a, "I'm good" and hit Mack on the shoulder. About 20 minutes later we pulled up to the ranch and saw a small tour bus unloading people. There were a lot of "touristy" looking people, a few had small children and they were loud. Really loud. "Lord I hope we don't have to sit in a class with them." I said to myself.

Two guys came out of the gift shop. One herded the bus crowd into the horse park and the other guy introduced himself as Juan. Juan was our private guide. He led us around the corner to a shaded area where we saw a few horses. A white horse, black horse and two bigger brown horses. He gave us a private safety and training class. He told us that we were not going the route of the other group.

We finished the safety course and picked our horses. Elise picked the black horse and Kellita picked the white horse. They then took a bunch of pictures with the horses and Juan. Mack and I went to our horses and took maybe five pictures. This was Kellita's first time on a horse and my second time. Elise has a friend with a stable in Atlanta that she goes to every few months and Mack grew up on a farm, so they were both very comfortable on horses.

I happened to turn towards Mack and he had a grin on his face. He pulled me to the side and said "Keep an eye on Kellita". I asked, "What for?" Mack told me to look at her outfit. Some shorts and a tube top? He wagered me $20 that one or both of her breasts would fall out of her top before the end of our excursion. He said they got into an argument over her outfit before they left the room, and she thought he was being insecure. I was not willing to take that bet at all! Her breasts looked like a D cup and I think I remember her saying she had a breast lift a few years ago. The possibility of one or both of them coming out was too high.

Juan got on his lead horse and we headed towards a trail at the back of the ranch. We went through a neighborhood and saw kids playing. They ran up to us waving and trying to sell us all kinds of trinkets. About ten minutes later, the woods opened up and we picked up the pace a little bit. It was a very peaceful ride. We were all just enjoying the beautiful views. I looked ahead to the ladies and could see them talking but I couldn't make out what they were saying. I could see Kellita kept adjusting her top and Elise was shaking her from head side to side. I could only guess what that conversation was about. Lala screamed at Juan a few times to slow it down a bit, so he did. Kellita couldn't hold onto the horse and her tube top too much longer. The trail we were on was kind of narrow. There were beautiful flowers and fruits along the way. We started going down a hill, then around another bend. I could smell and hear the ocean. A few minutes later the trees went away and I could see the beach about 100 yards away.

Between us and the beach was a steeper hill. Juan turned around and told us that the horses walk along this hill all the time. We just needed to trust our horses and hold on. Kellita looked scared, but Elise assured her that she would be OK as we headed down the hill. The hill twisted and turned with branches and loose rocks everywhere. The trail opened to a beautiful white sandy beach. There was no one on the beach and it seemed like it went on forever. Juan turned around and told us that we were going to go for a fast ride down the beach and then go into the water for pictures. I rode up next to Juan and told him that he could not take pictures of the men and ladies together. He nodded his head and we let the ladies go out first. I turned to Elise, she looked stunning and so natural on her black horse. Juan followed her on his horse while taking pictures. Elise went down about 50 yards and back and then led her horse into the water. Juan got off his horse and took more pictures of Elise. She jumped off the horse and into the water and did different poses. She was feeling that photo shoot.

Elise rode up next to me, gave me a high-five and leaned in for a kiss. Now it was Kellita's turn. She went kind of slow at first but came back faster. Faster was bad for her coming back though. Her top flipped down. She didn't notice at first, but Juan did. Juan was steady taking pictures. Mack was cracking up on his horse. Juan gestured at his chest and it took her a few seconds to get what he was saying before she stopped the horse and adjusted herself. While Kellita was off her horse, she went on to take more pictures in the water. Mack wiped the sweat off his face and slapped the back of my horse and I took off down the beach. I was not ready for that, so I hung on for dear life and tried not to fall off. I finished my short photo shoot and rode back next to Elise. Mack took off like he was in the Preakness. He was standing up on his horse and went from side to side. He looked natural on his horse. We could tell he had been on a horse many times. When he got back Juan gave him a high five and hug. Then we all headed back to the ranch.

Kellita immediately punched Mack in the arm when we got back to the ranch and he laughed it off. Then she came up to me and told me to never speak about her breasts popping out and pinched me. Elise came over and grabbed me tight and told me she loved the way I handled my horse. It made her feel some type of way. We went into the gift shop and screened the photos that Juan took to make sure that it didn't look like a baecation. We then headed back out to the van.

Elise grabbed my hand and pulled me into the van towards the back. We drove down the street and Elise moved over with her back to the window. She then started taking off her shoes and shorts. Elise looked me in the eyes, grabbed my chin and put my face between her legs. After a few minutes, she tensed up, grabbed the back of my head and let out a quiet sigh. I sat back up and grabbed my water bottle to splash my face. Mack and Kellita were up in the captain's chairs blasting some music, oblivious to what just went on in the back. When we got back to the resort, Mack and I went to the bar to grab some cold beers while the ladies went up to get ready for the all-white sunset cruise.

We met by the bar for drinks before we headed to the sunset cruise. Elise and I had matching outfits. I had on white linen shorts, a white linen shirt and white boat shoes. Her dress fell a little below the knee, it fit her loose with a nice neckline and spaghetti straps. Her dress also had pockets which she constantly reminded me of by twirling. Her hair was in a ponytail with a large white bow.

Mack and Kellita both had on white linen shorts and matching light blue golf shirts. Kellita's hair was in a ponytail with a white bow as well. Mack had on white Chuck Taylors. The front desk clerk offered to take pictures. The ladies went to the side and took about a dozen pics then the desk clerk took a few of Mack and I.

Our van pulled up and we hopped inside. We talked about the horse ride and how much fun it was. About thirty minutes later we pulled up to the marina. There were some gorgeous pieces of machinery in the marina. We found our yacht. It was gorgeous and was one of the bigger yachts in the marina. The ocean was calm and the sky was still clear. We boarded the boat after taking a few pictures and were greeted with a hot towel and champagne. The crew member extended a plastic bag with our names on it and asked us to drop our phones in for the duration of the cruise. They would have two photographers and a videographer on board the yacht. He led us to the bar and handed us non-disclosure agreements. We all signed, he then told us there were a few more guests arriving and that we should make ourselves comfortable anywhere because we would will be off shortly.

We found a couch and chilled out with our champagne. The next couple that came aboard looked familiar. Elise said that he was the lead actor in the last movie we saw. He looked a bit older in person. His wife looked much younger. He shook everyone's hand and took pictures. He seemed like a cool down to earth guy. The next couple that came aboard was a popular R&B singer and a woman I didn't recognize. They both wore white bikinis, fishnet pants with cover ups and Adidas. A few moments later the yacht pushed off.

The music started and we could smell the food cooking. A crew member walked around and took drink orders. Elise and I cuddled up on the couch and looked over at the ocean. I looked up and Mack motioned for me to come up to where he was but I preferred to chill out here with Elise. A photographer snapped our picture and then walked away. Elise felt me try to get up so she told me that we would have a chance to go over all the pictures and delete any we didn't like before we left the boat. I relaxed, she put my legs on her thighs and rubbed my calves.

The sea was calm, the drinks flowed, the music was great, and the atmosphere was very good. Everyone enjoyed themselves. Elise saw another couch open-up closer to the front of the yacht and we went up there and mingled with the other guests. After a few moments of chatting, we went back to see Mack and Kellita at the back of the yacht where there was a hot tub. Mack was shirtless and Kellita did not look happy but let Mack be Mack. Mack sat on the edge of the hot tub with his feet in. There were a few women topless in the hot tub with him drinking champagne. Kellita was behind Mack sipping her drink and chair dancing to the music. Mack turned around and she pointed at herself then the other women to remind Mack that she was one of the top three women on the yacht and he needed to behave accordingly. Mack smiled at her and nodded his head but then turned around and mingled with the women in the hot tub.

We felt the yacht slowing down and looked over to see a platform floating by itself in the ocean with tables set up for dinner. Flowers and fruit were everywhere. The captain paused the music to tell us we would be disembarking and eating dinner on the platform during sunset. The yacht turned around so the aft was next to the platform and we got ready to get off the yacht.

A crew member tied the yacht to the platform then lowered a plank. We all walked onto the platform and saw that we had assigned seats. Elise and I happened to be sitting across from the famous movie couple. Mack and Kellita were at the opposite end of the table. The crew members connected a few cables and then the platform was filled with low light and soft music. The sun was beginning to set as the waiters handed everyone a glass of champagne to toast. A few moments later we watched the sun go down and toasted. Just as the sun went down, the lights became brighter and more upbeat music started playing.

The dinner was on point. There wasn't a cloud in the sky and plenty of stars were visible since we were far away from the city lights. Dinner was winding down, everyone was laughing, eating dessert and enjoying themselves. Then we heard a glass break at the other end of the table. We all looked that way and saw that Kellita had her finger in Mack's eye. All I saw was her neck moving back and forth. Mack had his hands up looking like he didn't do anything. She threw her drink in his face and pushed him so hard that he lost his balance and fell into the water. I almost got up but Elise put her hand on my shoulder. I looked back and Mack was standing neck deep in the water. He swam past us to the yacht and a crew member helped him up. There were a few moments of silence after he got on the yacht and then everyone went back to what they were doing. A waitress came around and handed everyone a hot towel and said we would be leaving in a few minutes and that we should make our way back on board. Elise asked me to go ahead of her and then she went to talk privately to Kellita on the platform.

Everyone was now back on the yacht. The music was pumping, people were dancing, and the drinks were flowing. I sat on a couch at the front of the yacht and mingled with some people. The movie star and his wife joined me on the couch and started a conversation. We were in the middle of talking about how Atlanta has changed when a crew member came up to them with an iPad and asked them to go through the photos and videos from the cruise. I leaned back and looked up at the stars while they scrolled through the photos.

I think I was about to doze off but then I felt a hand go through my hair. It was Elise smiling at me. The famous couple finished going through their photos. The wife complimented Elise on her dress and the crew member handed us the iPad. Elise and I looked through and carefully made our selections. Elise kept a lot of the photos with herself and Kellita. We did see a photo we needed deleted. It was the one of Elise laying between my legs, eyes closed, holding a wine glass. It looked great to us, but we couldn't risk the chance of it getting out and possibly destroying our secret.

We were still sitting on the couch looking over at the water when we heard some laughter coming from the back of the yacht. Mack and Kellita came to the front holding each and laughing loud. I looked up at Elise. She leaned in and whispered to me that she had a talk with them and everything was good to go. Elise also said not to talk to Mack about it ever. We all sat on the couch and listened to the music while looking up at the stars on the way back to the marina.

I can't help but think about what happened with them the two of them at the dinner though. I remember there was a very nice- looking Latina lady sitting across from Mack. Kellita was on his right. There was an older white dude on his left. I remember a Latina chick was kind of flirty and she was also one of the topless ladies in the hot tub before dinner. Maybe she was playing footsies under the table with Mack and Kellita saw it and lost her mind.

We returned to the marina and said our good-byes. This was our last night and it was past midnight when we arrived back at the resort. Elise suggested we put on some swimsuits and go to the beach for one last swim. We all got changed and met back on the beach. The water was warm but choppy. We decided not to go out too far. We just found some lounge chairs and put them in the water. We listened to the ocean while looking up at the stars. This was a great vacation. Kiesha did a great job.

The next morning, I woke up and ran my hand up and down Elise's legs. I kissed her shoulders and squeezed her tight. The sun peeked thru the blinds and the ocean air warmed up the room. Elise turned around and wrapped her legs around mine. Her soft breasts pressed against my chest and she kissed me. "I need one more day like this with you" she whispered. Elise reached down and put me inside her. She rode me for a few moments then rolled onto her back. "This is how every couple should start their day" I said. Elise bit her lip and told me to go deeper and faster. She grabbed my waist to help me go deeper. Elise pushed me off of her and went to the chair by the bed and bent over it. I hopped out of the bed and gave Elise as much of me as I could. The chair scraped the floor and she moaned with every stroke until I came inside of her.

We met Mack and Kellita downstairs for lunch before we

headed to the airport. Elise and Kellita took a bunch more pics on the way out of the resort. They had the van stop at a few little shops on the way to pick up gifts. Our flight was on time and the weather report was nice for Atlanta. Mack and Kellita seemed cool now, like nothing ever happened. I wish I could just get a clue as to what went on at dinner last night, but I had to let it go. We boarded our flight and took off for Atlanta.

All of us are in first class getting ready to disembark and now our baecation rules go into effect. Mack and I let the ladies get off first and waited a few minutes to get some separation. Never know who you will meet in the Atlanta airport, so we had to be careful. Mack and I got off and walked slowly towards baggage claim. We talked about the ladies and how great the trip was. I was still trying to figure out what the hell happened at dinner, but I couldn't ask him. I got a call from my wife so I stopped to answer and Mack gave me the peace sign. We dapped each other up and he went on ahead. I stopped to get a smoothie and chatted with my wife. I told her I would be staying in Atlanta a few more days and to send me some properties she wanted me to look at. My wife said she was going to be in Vegas with her sister for a few days so no need to hurry home to her. I could spend extra time in Atlanta and possibly hang out with Elise once or twice.

I stopped to get a lotto ticket near baggage claim and spotted Elise getting her luggage. She saw me and smiled. Kellita's husband came to take them home. They grabbed their bags and headed off. I let them get out of the door and went to get my luggage. I took my bag off the conveyor belt and spotted Mack talking to some older white guy by the MARTA entrance. They stood a little too close for comfort in my opinion. The white guy had Mack's carry-on bag in his hand and I thought that was odd as well. Then the white guy grabbed the back of Mack's neck and kissed him in the mouth. I swear time stopped for me. I stood there with my mouth wide open. What in the world? Mack is bi-sexual? I never had a clue and I didn't get that vibe from him at any time. How? When? Why? I found the nearest chair and sat down. So many thoughts ran through my head. I reran the whole vacation in my head. Then a light went on. During the dinner cruise, could it have been the white guy and Mack at dinner and not the flirty Latina chick? Mack and the white guy were still there talking to each other. Mack was holding the white guys face like he was about to kiss him again. They embraced and headed into the MARTA entrance.

I texted Elise since I knew she wasn't driving and told her what I saw. She responded with a bunch of smiley faces and a meme of a person laughing in a salon chair. She texted that I may as well know what happened at the dinner cruise since. Elise said that the white guy that was next to Mack at dinner was fondling him under the table. Kellita said she went to rub Mack's leg and felt another hand down there and lost her shit. Mack told her he liked men as well after about a month of them sneaking around. On this vacation Kellita specifically asked Mack not to show that side of him. I texted back a "crazy" meme. I told Elise that I was spending a few days in town to look for a house and was going to get a hotel near her home. Elise sent back a heart emoji and said she would get her assistant to carve out some time for us the next day. I sent a bunch of hearts back as I walked to the rental car counter.

What a way to end a baecation?

I would like to say thanks for reading my book. This was especially challenging. I had to get over myself and sit down and write. Thanks to my editor for laying down a framework for me to go back thru my work. A very special thanks to my friend who kept me motivated to stay the course. Thank you as well to those few people who I shared this with before it was published. If you don't have a great village, then move to another one.